ELLA AND PENGUIN
A PERFECT MATCH

By Megan Maynor
Illustrated by Rosalinde Bonnet

HARPER
An Imprint of HarperCollinsPublishers

Penguin held up a pair of pants.
"Aha! These are just right!"

Ella twirled into the
room in a tutu.

"Ta-da!"

"Oooh!" said Penguin.
"So poufy!"

"You should wear one too!" said Ella.
"Then we will match!"

"Do we want to match?" asked Penguin.

"Of course!" said Ella. "We're friends.
And friends match!"

Penguin dropped the pants and stepped into a tutu.

He wobbled and wiggled.
He twisted and turned.

He breathed in
more than out.

pfff!

"Look at us!" Ella flung an arm around Penguin.
"So matchy matchy!"
"Uh-huh," said Penguin.

"Come on. Let's get a treat!"
Ella peeked into the cupboards.

"Do you like peppermints?"
"Do you?" asked Penguin.

"Oh, yes!" said Ella.

"Then I do too!" said Penguin. "Because
we're friends! So we match!"

"Mmm-mmm-mmm!" said Ella.

"Yow," said Penguin. "Hoo boy!"
He breathed out like a dragon.
"Haaaaah! Hehhhhhh! Huuuuuh!"

"Hey, Penguin, want to finger paint?"

"Um . . ."

Ella was nodding.
So Penguin nodded too.

"Another match!" said Ella.

"That's us. Matchy matchy."
Penguin waddled after Ella
in his too-tight tutu, fanning
his minty breath.

Ella and Penguin dipped into the paints.
"Oooh!" said Ella.

"Ew," said Penguin.

Ella dabbed and dashed.

She swooshed and swished.

"Look at this one!" Ella held up a painting.
"It's called *Apple Tree Man.*
    "And this one is called *Flower Parade.*
    "And this one is *Lasagna Qué Pasa!*

"What's the name of your painting, Penguin?"

"I don't like finger paint."

Ella laughed. "That's a funny title. Let me see."

"Oh," said Ella. "You don't like finger paint."

"It's too slimy," said Penguin.

"And peppermints are too minty."

"And this tutu is TOO TOO TIGHT!"

"I will miss being your friend,"
said Penguin. *Sniff.*

"I will miss being your friend,"
said Ella. *Sniff. Sniff.*

Sniff. Sniff.

Ella peeked over at Penguin. "It's hard to match all the time, though, right?" Penguin nodded. "Very hard."

"Maybe we could just match *sometimes*," said Ella.
"Like on Thursdays?" said Penguin.
"Or . . . whenever we actually like the same things," said Ella.

"Oh, I see," said Penguin. "So you could wear
the tutu and I could wear something *different*?"
"Yes," said Ella. "What do you want to wear?"

Penguin leaned in close.
"Pants."

"Um . . ." Ella looked at Penguin's legs.
"Are you sure?"

"Positive!" said Penguin.
"Be right back!"

"Oh, Penguin, I love your long hair."
"Why, thank you."

"Look at us," said Ella. "So un-matchy matchy!"
"Because friends don't always match," said Penguin.
"Of course not," said Ella.

Whee!

For Jeremy, my perfect match
–M.M.

For Galatée
–R.B.

Ella and Penguin: A Perfect Match
Text copyright © 2017 by Megan Maynor
Illustrations copyright © 2017 by Rosalinde Bonnet
All rights reserved. Manufactured in China.
For information address HarperCollins Children's Books, a division of HarperCollins Publishers,
195 Broadway, New York, NY 10007.
www.harpercollinschildrens.com

ISBN 978-0-06-233089-5 (trade bdg.)

The images for this book were created with watercolor and pencil on Hot Press, High White
watercolor paper, 200 lb., Saunders Waterford, and finalized in Adobe Photoshop.
Typography by Erica De Chavez
16 17 18 19 20 SCP 10 9 8 7 6 5 4 3 2 1
❖
First Edition